Sally and the leaves

A Harcourt Achieve Imprint

www.Rigby.com
1-800-531-5015

"Here is a red leaf,"

said Sally.

"Here is a yellow leaf,"

said Sally.

"Here is a brown leaf,"

said Sally.

"Look at the leaves!"

said Mom.

"Here is the red leaf,"

said Sally.

"Here is the yellow leaf,"

said Sally.

"Here is the brown leaf,"

said Sally.

"The leaves are for you,"

said Sally.